LADDIE
OF THE LIGHT

By Jane Briggs-Bunting
Illustrations by Jon Buechel

Another book by Jane Briggs-Bunting
with Jon Buechel
Whoop for Joy A Christmas Wish

Black River Trading Company
    P.O. Box 7
    Oxford, Michigan 48371
    810-628-2986
    Fax: 810-628-6422

Printed in the United State of America by Worzalla Printers/Binders

Publisher's Cataloging-in-Publication
    (Prepared by Quality Books Inc.)

Briggs-Bunting, Jane, 1950-
    Laddie of the Light / by Jane Briggs-Bunting,
    Illustrations by Jon Buechel
    p. cm.
    Summary: A little girl comes to terms with her parents' divorce during a
    summer spent with her grandfather and a special dog named Laddie.

    Preassigned LCCN: 97-93003

    ISBN 0-9649083-1-X

    1. Divorce--Juvenile fiction. 2. Great Lakes--Juvenile fiction. 3. Shipwrecks--
    Great Lakes--Juvenile Fiction. I. Title.

PZ7.B76435L3445 1997   [Fic]
                                        QBI97-40170

To my husband, Robert,
and all the wonderful dogs, cats and other critters
who have shared our life together
and, of course, Trapper and Laddie
                    -Jane Briggs-Bunting

To Shirl, a wife
in a million
                    -Jon Buechel

Chapter 1

Jesse felt miserable. She couldn't talk to anyone about her problem. She was too embarrassed, too ashamed. It must be her fault. She'd thought and thought, but she still wasn't sure what she had done to make something this terrible happen.

And her stomach...it felt like it did after she'd eaten too much turkey with stuffing and pumpkin pie on Thanksgiving, or the time she'd had three candy apples, two corn dogs and gone on a roller coaster at an amusement park. But the feeling didn't go away. She just felt sick all the time.

School was awful, too. She used to like school, but she didn't feel like laughing and giggling like before. It was hard to pay attention. Her teacher, Mrs. Brooks, had frowned at her a couple of times when she hadn't done her homework or didn't know the answer. Jesse had always done her homework and studied hard. She couldn't seem to concentrate on school work now. The words in her book would just blur. Her mind was too busy thinking about what had gone wrong.

Divorce. It was such an ugly word. Mom and Dad had

been yelling at each other a lot. She'd heard them both say the word a couple of times. Sometimes her mother was in tears. Sometimes one or the other of them would just leave and not come back for awhile...a day, maybe two or three. She was afraid sometimes that they'd both leave and forget she was here.

She wished she could talk to Jason. He'd know what to do. He'd been through it. He was her brother, half brother really. They had different dads. Jason was special. He could be absolutely impossible, of course. He'd tease her a lot and when they were little, they'd argue. But he was better than her friends' older brothers. Before he left for college, he'd help her with homework when she was having problems, take her out for a hamburger or just an ice cream cone so they could talk...really talk. He was away at school and wasn't coming home this summer. He'd gotten a job and was thrilled he could stay in his apartment with his friends. She couldn't mention it to him on the phone with her mother on the other line or in the same room. She could call him, but bills, including the phone bill, were one of the topics her parents argued about, mostly at night, when she was in bed.

No, she'd have to deal with this herself. Some of her friends' parents had divorced. Several had moved and couldn't go to the same school any more. That would be awful! Some had new fathers or mothers, sometimes even new brothers or sisters. She felt sick again...she had to figure something out.

Then June came and school was out, and her parents got rid of her. There was no other way to describe it. They told her that she was going to spend the summer up north with her grandfather in his cottage on the lake. He was lonely, they said, because, Nanna, grandpa's wife, had died last fall.

She'd have a wonderful time, they said. Nobody asked her what she wanted. She wanted to play baseball this summer and go swimming with her friends. She wanted the whole summer to work on keeping her family together. Now she was to be banished up north with Grandpa!

"I love Grandpa," she told them. "But he's so old! He won't understand me, and he can't rollerblade, and he won't like listening to my music...or anything. I'll die of boredom!"

Then, Jesse couldn't help herself, she just blurted it out, "Are you getting a divorce?"

Her parents just looked at each other. Neither knew what to say. Then her father said, "You'll always be my little girl." And Jesse knew it was true.

"What did I do? I'm sorry...I'll be better..." Then, Jesse started to cry.

"It's not you, Jess, it's us," said her mother softly. She was crying, too. So was Dad.

"We don't know for sure what is going to happen. That's what we have to figure out in the next couple of months. Your mother will be up some weekends, I'll try to get up to see you, too. You're a big girl. You're almost a teenager. We know you can handle it," he said.

Then her mom added, "You've always loved it up at the cottage. Grandpa calls you his mermaid. You can swim every day, and there'll be other kids to play with. It'll be a lot of fun.

Grandpa's really looking forward to having you. It's been lonely for him, Jess."

And that was that.

So here she was, cast-off, abandoned. She and Mom had come for the weekend. Her mother had left Sunday. Grandpa had looked at her teary face as her mother drove away and told her, "It won't be so bad being stuck with an old man! We'll have fun. I promise."

Grandpa had been really nice. Together they drove into the tiny town nearby for ice cream. He took her fishing in his boat and even baited the hooks for her. He taught her how to use the small skiff and told her she could take it to explore the various beaches along the coast. However, she always had to wear a life preserver and stay within sight of the shoreline. In the evenings, he played checkers and board games with her. His fat orange tiger cat, Trapper, had chosen to curl up and sleep each night, leaning in the curve of her knees as she slept on her side. His purring distracted her thoughts and lulled her to sleep.

Her favorite nights were when Grandpa told her stories of the "really old days," as she teasingly called them. She could get lost in them.

He told stories of the sailing ships and steamers that plied the waters of the Great Lakes and of ferocious northeasterly gales like the late season blizzard of May 18, 1894, that sank dozens of ships on Lake Michigan including schooners with names like M.J. Cummings, Moses Gage and Lem Ellsworth and steamers named Hudson and E. S. Tice.

He described in vivid detail the wreck on August 30, 1880 of the passenger steamer, Marine City, in Lake Huron where at least nine drowned when sparks from the steam engine's boiler set fire to a load of cedar shingles. The life saving crew from Sturgeon Point Lighthouse had been off picking berries when the ship caught fire!

He also told stories of the years before the great ships when the Sauk and Chippewa Indians lived in the region long before the white settlers. He described towering pines and plentiful game for hunting and fishing and told of the pure clear streams and birch bark canoes the Indians used to paddle up and down the coast. He told of sacred circles of stones used for religious ceremonies as the Indians sought to placate the gods who made the thunder rumble across the bay or brought plentiful harvests of fish and successful hunts for deer.

He showed her a shoe box full of arrow heads, amulets and fire stones, pieces of pottery, and rocks with pictographs that he had found in this area during his own explorations as a boy and years later as a man.

Listening to his stories, her stomach didn't hurt so much. She could picture his vivid tales in her mind before she fell asleep with Trapper softly purring next to her.

Chapter 2

Three days a week, Grandpa worked at the lighthouse about a mile south of the cottage. He worked as a volunteer either in the lighthouse museum or as a helper in the adjacent gift store. Many visitors stopped to see the old keeper's cottage and tower. He had taken the first week of her visit off, but now he had to return. Grandpa asked if she wanted to volunteer with him, but she hadn't really wanted to. Not now. Not yet. He said he understood.

Jesse remembered how two summers ago, she had climbed to the top of the lighthouse with Mom, Dad and Jason. It had been scary to be so high up at first, but it was fun, too. It was so clear she could see the water stretching out to meet the sky, and two sandy crescents curving away from each side. A huge freighter was going by and lots of other boats, too. They'd all been so happy...then.

Suddenly, the lump was back in her stomach and one had started in her throat, as well. "I'm not going to cry again," she whispered fiercely to herself. "I need to keep busy...Maybe I should have gone with Grandpa." She headed down to the beach and saw the skiff sitting near the edge of the sand.

Jesse raced back to the cottage, put her swimsuit on under her shorts and t-shirt, grabbed a sweatshirt, her life jacket, a beach towel and packed herself a lunch. She put everything in the skiff, then pushed the little boat into the water. She climbed on board a little awkwardly, swinging her leg over the side, wriggling the rest of herself on and belly-flopping to the bottom. With a few pulls, she started the little engine and guided the boat northward, away from the lighthouse.

The weather was sunny but a little chilly on the open water. She slipped on her sweatshirt, then put on the life jacket, pulling her baseball cap with its long visor snugly onto her head.

The beach was nearly deserted. Her grandfather was one of the few year long residents. Many of the summer people and renters had not yet arrived. The Great Lakes took their time shedding their ice and warming in the summer.

She piloted the little boat through several bays, careful to keep just inside of the sandbar that stretched out for almost a half mile or more in places.

Jesse kept going until there were no more cottages, just what seemed like miles of narrow, empty beach with towering white pines behind.

The water was clear as glass and very shallow, but the soft, forgiving beach sand of her grandpa's bay was gone. This stretch of coastline was strewn with boulders and rocks. Carefully, she picked her way to shore, the engine kicked up almost out of the water. Sometimes the bottom of the skiff scraped a rock. She cut the engine, pushed the boat ashore and wrapped the anchor and line around a small tree so the boat wouldn't drift off.

Excited, she felt like Magellan or Columbus exploring a new world. Carrying her lunch with her she set off to explore, her sandaled feet slowed by the soft, golden sugar sand. She found dozens of fossilized pebbles known as Petoskey stones, and lots of other fossilized rocks. She also discovered a smooth piece of stone with printing on the back—it looked like a shard of pottery!

Shipwrecks! There'd been hundreds along the coast over the years, and some had lost cargoes of silver dollars and gold—at least according to her grandfather's stories. She sat down to eat her lunch and afterwards decided to explore more of the forest that bordered the woods. Maybe she'd find an arrowhead...buried treasure...gold doubloons. Then she chuckled to herself. It was the wrong area for gold doubloons. The Spanish never made it into the Great Lakes!

Jesse lost all track of time in the woods as she searched using a stick to prod beneath the sand floor under the pine needles.

She didn't notice the heavy fog rolling in from the lake, shrouding the coastline, deadening the splash of the water on shore. The fog darkened the woods. Chill, moist air that touched her bare legs finally made her aware of the change in weather.

"Better get back to the beach," she said to the trees

around her. "I can find my way back by hugging the shoreline close and going back the way I came."

But finding the beach seemed impossible. She couldn't recognize any landmarks. The trees all looked the same, ghostly sentinels barring her way. She'd wandered in her explorations further than she had thought, or the fog had confused her sense of direction, and she was going the wrong way.

"Stay calm, stay calm, don't panic," she told herself out loud. "Maybe," she thought, "if I listen carefully, I'll hear the lake."

Hard as she listened, however, she couldn't hear the lake, and she could barely see much beyond her outstretched arm. She wasn't sure of the time. Grandpa would be home just before 5 o'clock. He'd worry if she wasn't there. She hadn't even left a note, but he'd notice the boat was gone.

She sat down on a fallen log and tried to think. She'd gotten herself lost.

She could keep walking in the woods, and, if she got lucky, she might stumble onto the beach. If the fog was so thick here, how bad was it on the beach? Could she find the skiff? Yes, she thought, I can by keeping the lake to my left.. First, though, I have to find the beach.

Jesse got up, then sat down abruptly...Maybe, she should wait...maybe, the fog would clear.

She did not know what to do, and she was scared. "I am so stupid!" she muttered to herself. She couldn't do anything right, no wonder her parents were splitting up, she thought. Tears brimmed and rolled past her eyelids and down her cheeks.

She curled up into a tight ball on her side and let the tears wash over her. Thoughts tumbled over each other in her mind as the tears flowed. "What if I die out here! They'll be sorry then. How could I be so stupid!"

Suddenly, she heard a soft snuffling sound close to her face. When she opened her eyes, a small black nose, sandy black whiskers and two brown eyes, were inches from her face. Then, a moist pink tongue gently licked a tear from her cheek.

She flinched.

Chapter 3

"Who are you? Where did you come from? Are you lost, too?" She asked the little dog in front of her.

He wagged his tail and licked her face again. "Euuw! Don't do that," she said, wiping her face where he'd licked her. She sat up, and he nuzzled his head into her chest, so she started ruffling his rough, longish black and tan coat. "You're a friendly fellow. What are you doing in the woods? Is somebody with you?" Jesse called out, but no one answered.

The little dog moved away, stopped and looked at her, then trotted partway back. He started off again, stopped and barked twice at her, as if to say, "Come on!"

Jesse got up, brushed off the pine needles and dead leaves and followed the dog. He led her through the forest, scooting under massive tree trunks where there was room and scrambling over others as Jesse hurried to keep up. Damp grasses and plants brushed her bare legs.

"Hey, wait up!" she said to the dog who seemed almost to disappear in the mist in front of her. Then she'd hear a sharp bark and follow it, and there he'd be waiting for her.

In hardly any time at all, she emerged onto the beach. The little dog sat perfectly still watching for her. He picked up one of the short sticks washed up on the coast, wagged his tail and trotted off, the water on his left. She followed him a little further and spied her skiff in the distance.

"You are a very clever fellow," she patted and praised the little dog lavishly. His eyes seemed to gleam at her with acknowledgement, and his tail thumped in the sand.

She ran to the boat, hauled in the anchor and pushed it onto the water. "Brrrr! It's freezing," she told the little dog who pranced back and forth on shore. He splashed into the water and dog paddled around, his pink tongue lapping as he swam. He made his way back to shore, gave himself a vigorous shake, then dropped rolling in the sand.

"Want to come?" she asked.

He wagged his tail, barked once, then turned, ears pricked as if he heard someone. Off he raced back up the beach, vanishing into the fog.

"Bye, whoever you are and thanks!"

Jesse clambered over the boat's side, started the engine and straining her eyes to see the boulders, she puttered out of the small bay. When she rounded the point staying close to shore, she emerged from the mist and the lake once again gleamed crystal clear with the sun brightly shining just above the tree line. She revved the little engine and retraced her route back to the cottage.

Grandpa was there in the kitchen when she arrived, "Hi! How was your day?"

"Super...I had a real adventure."

Her grandpa looked curious, "Get into some jeans, clean up and you can tell me all about it over dinner. How does spaghetti sound?"

"Great, I'm starved!" Jesse said, and realized she was hungry for the first time in what seemed like months. Over dinner she told him about her explorations, the sudden fog and the small dog. "He looks like Toto, you know, the dog in the Wizard of Oz."

"Does he wear a plaid leather collar?"

"I think he had a collar. I didn't notice what it looked like. Do you know him?"

"Maybe, I do. How about if I tell you a story tonight about the really, really old days?"

After dinner, Jesse curled up in a big overstuffed chair near her grandfather's. Because the weather had turned colder, he had built a fire that crackled and hissed in the stone fireplace. The scent of the cedar logs perfumed the air. She watched the flames dance as the story began. Her grandpa's deep voice filled the room.

Chapter 4

"Along time ago, more than a century, when tribes of Indians like the Sauks, Chippewas and Ottawas still hunted and fished this region and roads were nothing but trails, the waters of the Great Lakes were the main means of transportation. Few lived inland other than those who harvested the great white pines.

"Just as now, tremendous storms used to arrive suddenly churning up the lake. For the ships on the lake and the people in them, the storms were treacherous and life threatening. Many a ship was smashed to bits on rock reefs as her captain tried to hug the coastline for safety. Many people lost their lives simply because they didn't know how to swim!

"The loss of so many lives and ships with their valuable cargoes lead the government to act, and Congress authorized the building of a series of lighthouses on the most treacherous rock points on the Great Lakes.

"Our lighthouse was built more than 125 years ago. The tower, a keeper's house, barracks and cottages for a complete life saving station were all built here on the point. The station was manned by surf men and equipped with large surf boats with long oars.

"One of the first lighthouse keepers was a man named Samuel Cooper. He kept the light, as they used to say. He'd keep the glass clean and the light operating all through the night and during bad storms. The surf men would patrol the beach for one mile on either side of the lighthouse, keeping a record of each ship as she passed and looking for problems in the event of storms or even fires. A lot of boats carried wooden shingles and boards from the lumbering camps. They had fire powered boilers, and sometimes the wood would catch fire from the sparks.

"The lighthouse keeper had several children including one daughter, Sarah. Women back then had lots of children, but a lot of babies died, too. During her last pregnancy, Sarah's mother died giving birth to a baby daughter. The infant died a few hours after her mother. Sarah was devastated by her mother's death and would walk for miles along the beach. Her brothers were older and all had jobs to do. Her grandmother had moved in with them to take care of the family. And though Sarah willingly helped out, she did not have a lot to do. She missed her mother terribly.

"One day while she was out walking and had gone a great distance, she sat down to rest and fell asleep. A heavy fog rolled in from the lake, and when Sarah woke she could not see her hand in front of her face. She got up, shook the sand from her skirt and, despite the fog, started walking back to the lighthouse.

"She knew her father would be climbing up the tower to

light the mighty torch to warn ships of the rocks on the point and guide them safely past.

"Then, out in the water, faintly, she could hear the clanging of a ship's bell. She peered out into the water, but could see nothing. She felt a freshening breeze on her face as the wind began to strengthen. She shivered a little when a cold blast hit her as tremendous winds swept in from the northeast. She could hear thunder rumbling in the distance.

"The winds blew off the fog, and she could see a ship foundering in the waves and hear its bell clanging for help.

"Picking up her skirts, she ran as fast as she could back toward the lighthouse. Though her sides ached and her feet seemed to stick in the sand, she raced on. Breathless, she spotted one of the surf men making his rounds.

"Sarah quickly told him about the ship. He hurried back to get the lifesaving crew, sending her back to where she'd seen the vessel. She was frightened. She could smell smoke. The ship was on fire! Flames were everywhere. Black smoke was carried on the winds to shore. The winds grew fiercer. Then the rains came down in sheets drenching her. She could hear the cries and screams of people on board the doomed ship. But monstrous waves were crashing on to shore.

"Finally, the life saving crew arrived, dragging the heavy surf boat with them. They launched it and pulled mightily on the oars, rowing to save the people on the now sinking ship. Sarah waded into the surging waves dozens of times, helping men, women and several small children out of the surf boat and leading them safely to the shore. Many women drowned,

their long, heavy skirts weighing them down in the water.

"Sarah spotted a basket bobbing in the water and thought she heard a muffled noise inside. She went out one last time into the waves and pulled in the basket.

"It was waterlogged and something inside was scratching furiously. She opened it up. Inside, wet and trembling, was a small, black and brown puppy with pointed ears and a rough coat. She picked him up and held him close to her chest. He was shivering but licked her chin weakly.

"She asked the dazed people on the beach if they knew who the puppy belonged to. No one had seen him before.

"Sarah took the pup back to the lighthouse and gave him some warm milk and fed him bits of meat she tore from a soup bone. One of the surf men, who was Scottish, told her the little dog looked like a Cairn Terrier. So, she named the puppy Laddie. He seemed to respond to it right away.

"Laddie stayed at the keeper's cottage. Sarah and the little terrier were inseparable. He'd follow her around like a shadow while she did her chores. He'd sit by her feet while she did her school lessons at night by lantern light, and he took great joy in finding sticks and branches big and small to drag out of the woods and lay at his mistress' feet so she could throw them for him to chase.

"His sharp ears heard many a boat in distress or a call for help long before the men on watch. The lighthouse keeper and the life saving crew came to trust his barking when there was trouble on the water.

"Inevitably, when he would go charging out, rushing

down the beach, plunging into the water, there would be something or someone in need of help.

"Sarah fashioned a collar out of deer hide. She had been lonely before Laddie came, now she was content... unless he decided to chew one of Papa's boots or dig in their garden. He'd get scolded, and she'd feel badly for not watching him better.

"Time passed, and Sarah was now 14 years old. She was small but strong for her age and could handle a small rowboat which she took out frequently, sometimes with her father or sometimes alone, to fish. Laddie could not go with her because he usually bounced around all over the boat, looking over the side and barking when she'd catch a fish and it would flop on the bottom of the boat. It was a great game to him, but once he almost tipped the boat over.

"Laddie would be left behind in the keeper's cottage or tied to a tree, or he'd race down to the water where he'd scan the horizon. If he could see Sarah's little boat, he'd plunge into the water and swim towards her. Twice he'd almost drowned, but Sarah had rowed the little boat with all her might to where she saw his head bobbing in the waves.

"One day, Sarah left for fishing. It was a beautiful summer day, just like today. She left Laddie tied to the small tree. He whined and complained, but Sarah patted him and told him to be good. She would be back soon.

"In mid-afternoon, the wind shifted suddenly to the northeast blowing a strong, cold breeze over the warm water of the lake. A dense fog rolled in so thick you couldn't see five feet in front of you. And the lake began to roughen. Laddie sat there and started to bark. Then he began to howl, and when the storm reached its most furious, he broke the deer hide strap that held him to the tree and went bounding off down towards the lake.

"Desperately the little dog raced up and down the beach, barking over the howling of the wind and smashing of the waves against the shore. Sarah's father, brothers and surf men went up and down the beach calling for her, but they could hear nothing except the crash of the waves.

"Suddenly, the little dog plunged into the water swimming furiously against the waves that kept forcing him back to shore. A wave seemed to swallow him.

"The next day, after the storm had quieted, two fishermen found the wreck of Sarah's boat on the shore almost five miles distant. A short distance away, weak and disoriented but still alive, they found Sarah holding tightly to her little dog. They carried her back to the keeper's house, but that night she began shivering violently. Pneumonia had set in. Laddie kept the vigil with Sarah's father and brothers staying by her bedside. There were no antibiotics back then which might have helped. She died several days later.

"That night a heavy fog again rolled in from the lake. Laddie started barking furiously, his tail wagging, scratching at the door of the keeper's house. Sarah's father let him out, and he charged down the beach. Others followed, knowing Laddie often heard cries for help before they did.

"One of the life saving crew swears he saw Sarah in the

distance and Laddie greeting her. Then the fog shifted, and the two simply disappeared. The next day her father found Laddie's collar in the sand. He buried it near a stretch of beach where Sarah and Laddie loved to play."

"Since that day, sailors and fishermen imperiled by storms or lost in fogs have sworn they've heard the sharp barks of a little dog leading them to safety. Up and down the coastline throughout the Great Lakes, children who are lost, desperately sad or lonely, have talked about a small dog with a rough tan and black coat who emerges from the white pine woods to play with them and, somehow, brings them to safety, peace and happiness once again.

"And once, in a great while, a few see a young girl in old fashioned dress calling him home."

Tears were silently sliding down Jesse's cheeks when her grandfather ended his story. "Why did she have to die, Grandpa?"

"Not all stories have a happy ending, honey. Life doesn't either. You just make the best of it."

She was silent for a while.

"Is it true, Grandpa? Could my Toto dog be Laddie?"

"I don't know the answer to either question, honey. It's a story I've heard through the years, ever since I was a little boy...Now I think it's past your bedtime."

Jesse went to sleep that night and dreamed vividly of Laddie and Sarah and wished it were all true.

Chapter 5

The next day, though she really wanted to look for Laddie, she stayed close to the cottage. Her grandpa said he wanted to get her a compass before she ventured out on the water again. "Fogs come up quickly on the lake. You have to be prepared," he said. "Laddie might not be around to help," he said, winking at her.

She cleaned the little cottage and even weeded the vegetable garden the next day, then walked down to the lighthouse with a picnic lunch to share with her grandfather.

Some of the ladies Grandpa's age made a fuss over her. He rolled his eyes at lunch when she teased him about them.

That Saturday they drove into a big city about an hour away, and Grandpa bought her two compasses, one to attach to her life jacket, the other she could to keep in her pocket. He showed her how to use them explaining the needle would always point north and she could gauge her direction from that.

They ate dinner in town and saw a movie before driving back home.

The next week, it rained on and off. Strong squalls stirred up the lake making further exploring impossible for awhile.

Jesse played in the waves surfing on a styrofoam board her grandfather had bought for her.

Jesse helped out at the lighthouse and on rainy afternoons she assembled puzzles, read books from the library, or listened to tapes she had brought with her.

Midweek, while she was drying the dishes with Grandpa, he cleared his throat, giving her a sidelong glance. "Your mom called while you were out."

"She did? When's she coming?"

"She asked how you were doing," he said, then paused. "She said to tell you she couldn't make it up this weekend. Something had come up at work."

"Oh," said Jesse, in a small voice.

"We'll have fun, Jess, don't worry."

"It's not that, Grandpa. I'm just worried about what's going to happen..you know...they may, uh, split up...divorce..." her voice trailed off.

"I'm worried, too, honey. But your mom and dad have to figure things out."

They were sitting reading a little while later when Jesse got up. "I'm kind of tired tonight, Grandpa. I think I'll go to bed early."

"I love you, Jess. So do your mom and dad."

"I know you do, Grandpa." But I'm not sure about Mom and Dad, she thought to herself. "I'm glad I'm here with you." And she went to bed, lying sleepless for hours even with Trapper's comforting presence in the crook of her knees. She slept late the next morning which dawned bright and clear.

Grandpa had already left for the lighthouse.

She cleared away her cereal bowl, made her bed and straightened up the cottage. She wrote a note for Grandpa, so he'd know where she was heading (she'd promised him she'd do so from now on). She packed a peanut butter and jelly sandwich, some cookies, an apple and extra bread to feed the gulls. Then, Jesse loaded the skiff and retraced her trip from last week to the empty stretch of beach, keeping a careful compass reading along the way.

As she slowly nudged the skiff toward shore, she was again mesmerized by the stillness and beauty. Beneath the clear water she saw a huge turtle swimming gracefully. She saw a pair of swans in the distance, and she watched in awe as they rose in flight—so different from ducks and the ever present Canada geese. A doe and her spotted twins were drinking at the water's edge. When they saw her, they bounded off to the safety of the trees.

Jesse plopped down on the sand and stared out into the water. Overhead, gulls shrieked and dove while the little sandpipers, as Grandpa called them, ran up and down the beach dodging the rolling waves.

She whistled a few times and called for Laddie. She felt foolish to have come looking for him. She sat down on her towel with a book, but she couldn't concentrate. Thoughts were tumbling over each other in her mind...she felt a mixture of hurt, anger, and sadness at her parents.

Both Mom and Dad had told her not to worry. They said everything would work out for the best. Yeah, best for whom?

Not for her, certainly. She wanted a full time mother and a full time father. She knew how hurt some of her friends were when their dad skipped a weekend visit or the awfulness when parents actually started dating! Yuck!

Suddenly, she felt a cool breeze and she sensed she was being watched. She looked up and there he sat. Perched motionless, staring at her was the small, bristle coated dog. As soon as he caught her eye, his tail started swishing on the sand.

"You're here! I...I was hoping you'd be here. Are you Laddie?"

The little dog gave a short bark and pranced towards her. He paused, turning back and pouncing at a stick in the sand. He picked it up, trotted back, dropping it in front of her. Then he sat down, cocking his head to one side, then the other. He clearly wanted to play. She saw the faded plaid collar.

"How did Grandpa know?" she asked the little dog. But then she remembered, the Laddie from the story had a deer hide collar. She had to ask him about that.

Jesse got up, picked up the stick and threw it down the beach. The two of them chased each other. Anything and everything was a toy to Laddie.

He pounced on a gull's feather, chased small stones that rolled on the beach, sniffed at a Daddy Long Legs scurrying along the sand. Jesse watched, laughing. Exhausted and hungry, Jesse sat down and the two shared her lunch. He even ate pieces of her apple.

They sat together, and gradually, as she watched the

clouds drifting past and absently petted his small head, she shared with Laddie her fears and worries about her parents, the divorce, what would happen to her.

Laddie just wriggled closer, putting his chin in her lap and sighing, occasionally licking her hand. She stroked his head, and the two sat there watching the antics of gulls and the patterns of the waves.

A gull's shadow swept across the sand, and the dog gave chase, finally looking up as the bird screeched and wheeled before plunging into the water to catch a minnow.

Jesse watched and marveled at the perfection of the day.

But in the distance she saw clouds on the horizon. The winds picked up pushing the clouds towards her, and she realized they weren't clouds at all but a fog. Then she heard the rumble of thunder to the north. She knew it was time to go home. She checked her watch (another purchase by Grandpa so she could keep track of time). It was after 4 o'clock!

Jesse looked at the sky. She'd always been a little bit afraid of thunderstorms. Laddie's ears pricked forward. His head cocked back and forth as he watched her. He raced to her boat, barking.

She shook the sand from her towel, picked up the trash from her lunch and loaded them in the boat. She called to him, and he trotted towards her. She patted his head. "Thanks for a lovely day,...and for listening...You're a good boy," she said.

Giving his head a final pat, she dragged the skiff back into the water. She picked her way through the rocks as the fog encircled her. She glanced back, and, though less than 20 feet from shore, it had already vanished.

Using her compass, she headed south. Once again, when she emerged from the mist, the lake cleared and the shoreline was easily visible. Only the isolated stretch of beach seemed to shimmer in fog.

But thunder did rumble again to the north, so she headed swiftly back to the cottage meeting her grandfather as he walked home from the lighthouse. He helped her pull the skiff up onto the shore.

"You okay?"

She nodded her head. "I saw him, again. It is Laddie. He had a plaid collar, just like you said. How did you know? I shared my lunch with him."

"That's a story for another night. We've got fireworks to watch tonight," Grandpa said.

"But it's not the 4th of July, Grandpa," Jesse said.

"You'll see," he promised. And she did.

That evening they watched Mother Nature's version of a laser light show as lightening bolts crackled and forked in the sky over the lake.

Much later, after they'd roasted marshmallows over the dying embers of a fire, the sky cleared.

To the north on the horizon, Jesse noticed shimmering curtains of blue and green lights. "What's that, Grandpa? Has the storm moved?"

"No, we're in for a rare treat. Your science teacher would tell you that's the aurora borealis. Folks up here call them the Northern Lights."

Chapter 6

The next day was Saturday. She headed the skiff back to "Laddie's beach", but it was different. Jet skis buzzed off shore like angry hornets. People carried coolers and towels and sat in chairs in the sun. There were lots of dogs, but she saw no sign of Laddie. She turned around and went back to the cottage and spent the rest of the day playing with several kids up for the weekend at neighboring cottages.

On Sunday, Jesse went fishing with Grandpa in the morning and in the afternoon helped him at the lighthouse museum's gift shop. She wrapped up visitors' purchases and answered people's questions, if she could. At the end of their shift she climbed with him way up to the top of the lighthouse tower. She wasn't as scared as before and leaning on the rail she could see for miles in each direction.

"Grandpa, do you know any other stories about this lighthouse?"

"As a matter of fact I heard one just the other day. Mabel told me about it when I mentioned your adventure with the little dog. I'll tell you tonight."

"Mmmmm, Mabel? The one who baked that pie we're

going to have for dessert tonight? I think she likes you, Grandpa!"

"Now don't you start teasing me, young lady!"

And the two joked and teased each other the entire walk home.

That evening, after a comfortable dinner of the perch they'd caught that morning (Trapper begging shamelessly from an empty chair at the table), Jesse settled again in the big overstuffed chair to listen to her grandfather.

He told another story about the wreck of the Pewabic right off their cottage where many had drowned, and the courtship of one of the lifesaving crew and a fisherman's daughter and how a little black and tan dog had brought them together.

As they were eating bowls of ice cream and a slice of Mabel's raspberry pie, she asked, "Oh, Grandpa. Can Laddie be real?"

"I don't know, Jess. But there's no harm in believing, is there? Right now, you have little enough to believe in, I suspect."

The next week, Jesse went back up the beach, carefully nudging her boat on to the now misty shore. The little dog was waiting. "Laddie! I love you!"

He picked up a stick, flipping it into the air then pouncing on it when it landed. His Christmas tree shaped tail wagging, he looked at her hopefully, picked up the stick, then dropped it next to her.

Jesse recognized the invitation to play. She picked up the

stick and tossed it a short distance down the sandy beach. The little dog chased after it, picked it up and returned to drop it at her feet. He sat down and looked up at her expectantly.

Jesse obliged and threw the stick again. The third time she threw it into the water, and Laddie pranced in, grabbed it and brought it back. The next time she threw the stick in deeper. The dog plunged in swimming out to the stick, carrying it back in his mouth. He trotted back onto the beach to Jesse, dropped the stick at her feet, then shook himself, sprinkling her with droplets of water.

"Ooh, that's cold!"

He tore off down the beach racing up and down. Dodging her outstretched hands, he bolted past her. At last, tiring from his exertions, he plopped down at her feet, rolled onto his back and exposed his belly for her to rub.

Then he sprinted off again. She whistled to get his attention then ran in the opposite direction. He chased after her up the beach, jumping at her shorts. She fell panting and they wrestled on the sand. Then he ran off again, barking as he chased the shadows of seagulls as they flew over the sand.

She picked up the stick and tossed it far into the water, well over the little dog's head. This time the dog danced to the edge of the water, looked at her, barked and sat down, tail thumping on the sand.

"Won't go? I expect you want me to get it for you?"

The dog barked, tail thumping, and Jesse raced in. "Ooh! It's cold. No fair, you've got a fur coat on!"

But when she turned around with the stick and headed

back to the beach, the little dog was gone.

She called and called, but he didn't come.

For the first time she noticed others arriving at the beach. It was Friday afternoon.

She shrugged, placed his stick high up on the sand away from the water and headed home. Maybe she'd see him again.

Jesse played with Laddie many days throughout the summer. Though she wanted to believe he was Sarah's dog come back to life, she knew that was silly. He probably belonged to someone nearby.

Her mother came up for several weekends.

Her father came up twice, and gradually she came to accept that her parents were divorcing. She sometimes felt angry at them, sometimes sad. Laddie became her confidant. Her stomach gradually stopped hurting.

Jesse learned to bait her own hook when she went fishing with Grandpa. She picked quarts of wild berries and even made a pie and jam. She became very good at answering questions about the lighthouse. She was content, but she worried when the end of the summer came what would happen to Laddie.

She had searched in the woods but could not find a cottage or people who owned the dog. On weekends, she'd ask folks who lived nearby. No one had ever even seen him.

Chapter 7

On her last week at the lake, she had a surprise visitor, her brother, Jason. He came for a visit with Grandpa and then to take her home.

"Oh, Jason. I'm so glad to see you. I've missed you," Jesse said as she gave her brother a hug.

"Hard to believe, but I've missed you, too," he teased, scrunching her baseball cap down over her eyes. Grandpa cooked burgers on the grill for lunch and they ate corn on the cob.

"You kids take the skiff out for a ride. Jesse, show him how good a captain you are. I'll handle the clean-up. I think Jess has missed her big brother."

The two headed out in the skiff, Jesse proudly piloting the little boat, showing off her skills to Jason.

"Grandpa's really cool," she told her brother. "He's an adult, but not like one somehow...He's fun!"

"Yeah, he is a neat old guy. I remember the summer I spent up here with him...I got a call from Mom. She told me about the divorce. Mom said it's been kind of hard for you."

"I'm okay, I guess."

"You know I remember when Mom and my dad split. I was younger than you, but I can still remember how I felt. It was awful. I kept trying to figure out what I'd done to cause the problem."

"You felt that way, too?"

"Yes, and I was just furious with both of them. I came up here that summer, and somehow, it all worked out...Mom eventually met Pete and he was a pretty okay guy. Then they had this puny, red-faced, funny looking, skinny..!"

"Hey, not fair!"

"Just kidding, then you came along, and I thought it would be happily every after. But it never is, you know? Change always happens. A lot of times, if you just let it flow, it all comes out for the best. You'll always have me and Grandpa, and Mom and your dad. Remember that. It'll just be different than it was, a little harder sometimes, but okay," he said reaching across to give her a hug that rocked the skiff.

"Yikes! You're going to dump us overboard," said Jesse.

"Feel the feelings, Jess. They're real to you. They're important. It's hard, but the sun's still going to come up in the morning and go down at night. The rest, well, it's unpredictable. It's just going to happen. Just don't let them put you in the middle or use you. Love them both. I'm finding out that the older I get I still don't know everything," he said, then stopped, a sudden grin coming to his face. "But don't tell Mom I said that!"

Jesse and Jason looked at each other and grinned in

perfect camaraderie.

They'd reached the stretch of beach where Jesse had played so often with Laddie. She surfed the boat right up onto the shore. Jason leapt out and pulled it up high onto the sand.

"Nice job," he said.

"Thanks! Come on, I've got something to show you," said Jesse.

Suddenly, they both spotted a small furry shape and a tail wagging like a flag.

"Laddie!" they both called in unison, then looked at each other.

The little dog poked his head up, whiskers covered in sand, then with a sharp bark raced down the beach towards them leaping enthusiastically from one to the other. He stopped, raced back and picked up his stick and dragged it down the beach to where they were.

"You know Laddie?" Jesse asked.

"I haven't seen him in years and years. But you know that summer I stayed up here with Grandpa? Well, I played with him almost every day. He's got to be awfully old. See, that's the collar I put on him. I replaced an old rawhide one that had almost worn through. Grandpa got it for me."

She stared at her brother, then he picked up the stick and tossed it for the joyful little dog. They played with Laddie until the sun started setting. Suddenly, his ears pricked forward and he turned around, and Jesse could have sworn she saw a little girl in old fashioned dress call to the dog and wave.

She blinked and looked again as Jason waved back. "It's

just Sarah, Jess. She's calling Laddie home. She knows you'll be okay now...Come on, Grandpa's got a surprise for you."

The two turned away and walked up the beach, got into the skiff and headed home to their grandfather's cottage, Jason's arm around his sister's shoulder.

Jesse turned to look back once, and she thought she saw a wagging tail disappear into the woods.

Back at the cottage, her grandfather was waiting.

"Did you tell her, Jason?"

"Nope, I thought you should."

"Your mother's already scolded me, but somebody dumped this little fellow at the lighthouse. I found him by chance a couple of days ago."

Jesse looked into the topaz eyes of a white and golden colored puppy with a white plumy tail, ears that flopped forward and a body too long for his short, stubby legs.

It was love at first sight. "Oh, Grandpa, he's adorable!"

"He's not a Cairn Terrier. In fact, he looks like he's got about a dozen different breeds in him. But he needs a home."

"He's for me?...Oh, Grandpa!...What did Mom say?"

"It's a done deal," said Grandpa and winked at Jason.

"He did some arm twisting..." said Jason laughing.

"Oh Grandpa! This has been the best summer ever!" And to Jesse's surprise, she really felt that was true.

"What will you name him...Laddie?"

"Oh, no, Grandpa. There's only one Laddie of the Light. We'll have to think!"

At that, Trapper jumped down from the chair where he perched staring unblinkingly at the puppy. He hissed once and stalked off, his tail erect. With a yip, the puppy bounded after him.

The End

Special thanks to Sally Tato and Erica Blake for their technical assistance, Curtis Wong for h photographs, Holly Shreve Gilbert for specialized help--twice, Erin Sims Howarth for publish ing guidance and to Wallis Andersen, Mary Hoisington and Carolyn Stevens for their help in critiquing and editing.

An extra special thanks to Betty Dobry for her candid criticism and helpful suggestions in th early stages of the manuscript.